A Very English Christmas

Also by Keira Andrews

Contemporary

The Spy and the Mobster's Son
Honeymoon for One
Beyond the Sea
Ends of the Earth
Arctic Fire

Gay Amish Romance Series

A Forbidden Rumspringa
A Clean Break
A Way Home
A Very English Christmas

Holiday

The Christmas Deal
The Christmas Leap
The Christmas Veto
Lumberjack Under the Tree (free read!)
A Baby for Christmas
Merry Cherry Christmas
Santa Daddy
In Case of Emergency
Eight Nights in December
If Only in My Dreams
Where the Lovelight Gleams
Gay Romance Holiday Collection

Lifeguards of Barking Beach

Flash Rip
Free Wind
Impact Zone

Sports
Only One Bed
Kiss and Cry
Reading the Signs
Cold War
The Next Competitor
Love Match
Synchronicity (free read!)

Valor Duology
Valor on the Move
Test of Valor
Complete Valor Duology

Fantasy

Barbarian Duet
Wed to the Barbarian
The Barbarian's Vow

Historical

Kidnapped by the Pirate
Semper Fi
The Station
Voyageurs (free read!)

Paranormal

Kick at the Darkness Trilogy
Kick at the Darkness
Fight the Tide
Defy the Future

A Very English Christmas

by Keira Andrews

A Very English Christmas
Written and published by Keira Andrews
Cover by Go On Write

Copyright © 2016 by Keira Andrews
Print Edition

ISBN: 978-1-988260-71-6

Acknowledgements

Thanks to my wonderful friends and beta readers Anne-Marie, Becky, and Jules. And thank you so much to the readers who are so passionate about Isaac and David. <3

Author's Note

This story takes place after *A Way Home*, the third book in the Gay Amish Romance Series.

Chapter One

"IT'S PERFECT."

They stood at the end of a little no-exit suburban street that backed up to a narrow stretch of land running along the railway tracks. Isaac's heart thumped. David was right—it *was* perfect.

"The garage would be just the right size," David added.

"It would. It's almost as big as the house." Isaac peered around. "It's quieter here at the end of the street. Except for the train, I guess."

David smiled slyly and leaned closer. His warm breath puffed over Isaac's cheek. "But we don't mind that particular noise, do we?"

Isaac flushed. Growing up in Zebulon, he'd dreamed of running away and riding a train all the way to the ocean. And on more than one icy Minnesota night, he'd pleasured himself to the train's distant rumble.

After checking the time on his phone, David

straightened the collar of his shirt beneath his jacket. "She should be here any minute." His pale blue eyes were bright in the way they got when he was excited about something. He ran a hand through his thick, dark hair, fiddling with the bangs that fell over part of his forehead.

They both wore button-up shirts and nice pants, although Isaac wished he'd put on a sweater as he shivered in the gray December gloom. "For California, it sure gets cold here sometimes."

David took Isaac's hands and rubbed them with a smile. "It hasn't even been a year yet, and we're getting soft. Just think of how cold the outhouse must be in Zebulon today. June said they already have a foot of snow. Maybe I'll get you some gloves for Christmas."

Isaac arched a brow. "We said we wouldn't buy each other anything. We need to save our money, or we'll never be able to move out. The gloves I have are perfectly fine. When I remember to bring them, that is." They both laughed.

"Yoo-hoo!" a woman's voice called. "Are you the boys I talked to about the rental?"

An older, redheaded woman approached from down the street, and David waved. "Yes, that's us."

"I'm Margery Hunt." She thrust out her hand, and David and Isaac introduced themselves. "Let me show you the place." She turned back up the street.

"Isn't it here?" Isaac pointed over his shoulder.

"Oh, are you interested in the house? I thought you answered the ad for the basement apartment." She opened a notebook and held it at arm's length, squinting.

"There must have been a mix-up," David said. "We need a place with our own garage. We saw the rental sign out in front of the house and thought that was it."

"That's for rent too if you'd rather." Margery scrawled something in her notebook. "The other house is divided into two apartments, but this one's a single. Two bedrooms and no basement, although you do get the garage. Of course the rent is higher."

Of course. Isaac's stomach clenched. "How much higher?"

"Fifteen hundred a month."

Isaac couldn't believe his ears. "It's fifteen hundred a month for the house?" They could afford that! They'd have to work hard, but—

"Sorry, kid. It's fifteen hundred *more*. Three thousand a month, and that's including utilities."

"Oh," Isaac said. He saw his own disappointment mirrored on David's face.

"Want to see it anyway?" she asked.

"Sure," David answered. To Isaac, he whispered, "Maybe it won't be what we want inside anyway."

"Maybe not." Isaac threaded their fingers together, and they followed Margery.

And of course the house was just as darn perfect

inside.

Despite the faded wallpaper and scuffed parquet floors, it was just what they needed. A regular-sized bedroom for them, a tiny bedroom where they could put a desk, a small kitchen, and a bathroom that needed new tiles and grouting. It wasn't fancy, or big, but it could be *theirs*.

Isaac held tight to David's hand as they peered around the good-sized garage where David could easily set up his workshop. There was even a storage shed in the backyard, which ended at the ridge before the railway tracks. It wasn't as if it was their *dream* house or anything. It was way too small, and the neighbors were too close for that.

Still, it would be years before they could afford to buy a place of their own, with land and perhaps a barn for a workshop and a few animals. Isaac still had to finish his GED, and college would be four years if he decided to go.

Margery had kept up a steady stream of chatter as she toured them around. "So that's about it. It's a great starter home for a young couple. What do you do?"

"We're both carpenters," David answered. "Although Isaac goes to school as well. It's an alternative school with flexible hours for students who are a little older."

Isaac added, "I'm still an apprentice carpenter. David does the designing too."

"Carpenters, hmm? That's a good trade. Do you make furniture and such?"

David nodded. "I've been fortunate to stay very busy since we moved here. Word of mouth has been good."

And fortunately for them, people in San Francisco were willing to pay huge amounts of money for custom furniture, cabinets, and fancy places to sit in the backyard called gazebos.

"Where are you boys from?" Margery asked.

"Minnesota," David answered.

Isaac knew she could hear the German in their accents but didn't explain any further. Most "English" people—as the Amish called anyone who lived in the modern world—were nice, although a few had treated Isaac and David like zoo animals once they found out they'd grown up Amish. Especially when they found out they'd lived in an ultraconservative sect that didn't even have indoor plumbing and had hardly any contact with the outside world.

At least now Isaac and David had learned a lot and could usually get by without being endlessly confused.

"Minnesota, huh?" She smiled kindly. "I hail from Wisconsin originally. My husband's people were from Modesto, so we ended up here in the Bay Area. Do you live in Dublin, or are you looking to move here from somewhere else?"

"Right now we're living in the city with my brother Aaron and his wife Jen," Isaac answered. "They have a town house in Bernal Heights. She's a doctor, and my brother teaches math." Why was he telling her that? *Focus and get to the point. People don't want your whole life story.* "It's been great living there, but we'd really like our own place somewhere a little quieter. We figured Dublin might be good since it's the end of the BART line and we can still get into the city." The online listing had said it was "steps" from the train station, although it was a fifteen-minute walk. But Isaac didn't mind.

"So you own two houses on this street?" David asked.

"Three, including the one my husband and I live in." She led them down the driveway and pointed to a bungalow with faded red trim and a fence that needed fixing. "It was his bright idea to buy these houses as rental properties years ago. I think it's time to sell them and stop being landlords. He's not convinced, even though his back has gotten so bad that he can't do much of the handyman work around the places anymore. So, what do you think? Can you take the house? If you've got your references and such, I can get the ball rolling today."

With shoulders slumping, Isaac and David shared a glance. Isaac said, "I think we'd better see the basement apartment."

DAVID STRIPPED DOWN to his briefs and stretched out on the bed with a sigh. He knew he had to let it go, but he couldn't get the house out of his mind. Before they got their dream house, they needed to find a place that would do in the meantime. The cramped basement apartment Margery showed them was…fine. They'd have neighbors upstairs, though, and David would need to find a space to rent for his workshop.

He'd hoped that if they could find an affordable house to rent with a garage, he could save money on the workspace and get a tax write-off—which he wasn't sure he quite understood, but it was apparently a benefit of working from your house. Most importantly, he could spend more time with Isaac.

Isaac had been working so hard between school and carpentry with David; if they could work from home, it would make it all so much easier. David loved the idea of not having to take crowded buses to his workshop.

Still, it didn't seem worth it to move out of Aaron and Jen's town house until the right place came up. Yet the more they looked, the more it seemed impossible to find anything in the Bay Area that was even in their ballpark. Even though he'd been putting away a bit every month to save for first and last months' rent, it wasn't enough.

Leaning a slim hip on the doorway to the adjoining bathroom, Isaac leered. "How you doin'?" He ran a hand over his sandy hair, which he kept short. After years with shaggy Amish haircuts, they both liked their hair neat and trimmed.

David waggled his eyebrows with a chuckle. They didn't always understand the jokes on TV, but Isaac loved that one from the show about friends. Lifting his arms over his head and keeping them in place, David wriggled down a bit on the mattress.

Isaac's eyes gleamed as he licked his lips. "Want it like that tonight?"

David nodded, anticipation sparking over his skin as the knot of anxiety in his chest unraveled. With Isaac he'd always been able to let go and be free, ever since the first night they'd tumbled to the forest floor in a rush of kisses and desperate release. When he gave Isaac control on nights like this, it was as if he was made new again, all the rough edges sanded away smooth.

With a few tugs and a kick, Isaac shed his T-shirt and plaid boxers. He straddled David's thighs, his balls rubbing over David's skin. Lips parted and breath coming shallow already, Isaac leaned over and pressed David's wrists to the mattress. "You know the rules."

"Uh-huh." David was getting hard already.

"I wish—" Isaac bit off his words and kissed

David. Their tongues slid together as they opened their mouths and slowly explored.

No matter how many times they kissed, David never got sick of it. Even though their kisses weren't furtive and forbidden anymore, the taste of Isaac's mouth and the scrape of his stubble still sent David's pulse skyrocketing and set his body humming like an engine. Isaac's breathy little murmurs and moans filled David's ears and flowed through him like water.

He broke the kiss. "What do you wish?"

Still holding David's wrists to the mattress, Isaac sat up. A flush crept up his neck, yet he didn't look away. "I wish we had our own bed that we made ourselves. With posts." He nodded to the gray padded headboard looming over them. "Not that this one isn't nice, but I want to…" He took a breath and blurted out the rest. "I want to tie you up. Only when we do it like this, and only if you want it."

Arching up his hips, David groaned. His cock strained in the confines of the cotton briefs. "That would be… Oh yes, I think I'd like that."

Isaac grinned and rubbed his thumbs over David's wrists. "You'd look so good, waiting for me." His smile faded. "I still don't want to hit you, though."

David laughed. "I don't want you to either. And I don't want to hit you."

"Lola said some people like to get whipped. Like,

for real! With actual whips and stuff. I don't get it."

Isaac's friend from school was a never-ending source of information about things that Isaac and David didn't understand. She'd sent Isaac some links about this "BDSM" stuff, and he and David had watched videos on their laptop with the sound down very low and their eyes extremely wide.

"We don't have to do anything we don't want to." David arched his hips again, needing friction and not getting it as Isaac still sat across his thighs. "When we have our own place, we'll definitely make a bed that you can… That you can tie me to." Saying it out loud made his heart skip.

Isaac's puzzled frown vanished, and he bit his lip. "And you'll lie there and do what I say." He leaned over again, his breath hot on David's ear. "What a good boy you'll be. *Mein guter junge.*"

A shudder rippled through David as he gasped. "Yes." Even though at twenty-three he was several years older than Isaac, in these moments he loved for Isaac to take charge.

Isaac let go of one of David's wrists to reach down and stroke him through his briefs. David didn't move, moaning. With his arms extended above his head and Isaac's weight over his thighs, he was deliciously trapped. Isaac kissed him roughly, and the thought of being actually tied down sent blood rushing in his ears.

They could design the posts and headboard so

that he could be bound with his arms straight above him, and also at the corners. Ideas and shapes flashed through his mind, and he almost wanted to stop and sketch the design.

An image flooded his mind—spread-eagled with his arms *and* legs restrained.

Crying out into Isaac's kiss, David bucked up. "Please, Isaac," he moaned. He'd sketch later.

"But I love you in your underwear so much," Isaac teased. Then he relented and kneeled beside David to tug the briefs off.

When David was free of them, Isaac grabbed the bottle of lube from the drawer in their bedside table and moved between David's legs. His arms still in place over his head, David lifted his knees to his shoulders. Sitting back on his heels, Isaac smiled, running his hands over the globes of David's ass. "Such a good boy." He bent over and sucked the head of David's cock.

The pleasure simmered in David's veins as he watched Isaac's cheeks hollow. He was so lucky to have this—to have Isaac. They did all sorts of things in bed together that David had dreamed of through lonely years. He loved fucking Isaac and being inside him. But sometimes it felt so good to let go of everything and open himself up to whatever Isaac wanted to do to him.

He'd always had so many responsibilities, and even though he and Isaac shared their burdens equally now, it still gave David such pleasure to give up all control and be…consumed.

Sucking hard, Isaac slicked a finger and teased David's hole before easing inside. He crooked his finger, looking for just the right spot, and when he found it, David shouted too loudly. Isaac stroked inside him and licked up and down his shaft. David pressed his lips together, inhaling sharply through his nose.

Aaron and Jen were upstairs on the third level of the town house, and David knew he and Isaac were too loud sometimes. How wonderful it would be to have their own house where they could scream and shout without being embarrassed in the morning. Not that Aaron and Jen ever said a word.

David clutched the fitted sheet with his fingers, his shoulders starting to twinge as he kept his arms extended. "Please, Isaac," he said, panting.

With a wet *pop* that sent a shiver through David, Isaac lifted his head. He pressed his palms against the back of David's thighs, pressing David's knees closer to his armpits. Isaac's amber eyes were dark, and he breathed hard. His faint freckles stood out on his flushed skin. "What do you want me to do?"

He grunted. "You know."

Isaac slicked his hand. "You want… You want me to shove my cock inside you?"

"Yes. Please." David watched Isaac pull down his

foreskin, the red shiny head of his cock appearing and then disappearing into his fist as he coated himself with lube. Neither of them were cut, and David was glad. He wanted every part of Isaac.

"You want me to fill you right up?"

Nodding vigorously, David wriggled his ass. There was something so obscene and forbidden about saying it out loud that excited them both. "Fuck me."

Isaac leaned over and kissed him hard before lining himself up and pushing inside. Neither of them had ever been with anyone else, and David was so glad they didn't have to use condoms. The burn of flesh on flesh curled his toes, Isaac's cock filling him.

David wanted to run his hands over Isaac's chest and scratch his nails through the hair scattered there, but he kept his arms above his head. They grunted when Isaac filled him all the way, his hips brushing David's ass.

"Oh, David." Isaac moaned. *"Du willst mehr, nicht wahr?"*

Yes, he wanted more. *"Ja. Tiefer."* Wanted it deeper.

Their skin slapped together, Isaac pumping his hips with one hand gripping David's shoulder and the other around his cock. "You feel so good. You're so tight. Just for me." Isaac closed his eyes and tipped his head back, fucking David hard.

"Just for you," David echoed with a grunt. "Always you."

"*Ich will dich so sehr*," Isaac muttered.

"I want you too."

His balls tightened, and David wondered what it would be like to have Isaac fuck him while wearing Amish clothes again. The orgasm ripped through him, and he cried out. Isaac clapped a hand over David's mouth, sending another surge of pleasure burning through him.

He splattered his chest, shuddering and gripping Isaac's cock with his ass. Nostrils flaring, he panted against Isaac's palm.

"Love you so much. You're so good." Isaac pounded into him, eyes wild as he arched his back and came, his head back and mouth open in silent ecstasy, shooting deep inside David.

When Isaac collapsed forward, he lifted his hand from David's mouth and kissed him softly. They were a sweaty, sticky mess. Even after almost a year away in the outside world, sometimes David could still hardly believe he was here with Isaac. That this was allowed.

Isaac stretched up his hands to grasp David's fingers and lower his arms. He pressed a wet kiss to each of David's palms, his breath hot. "Just think of how good it will be in our own bed," he murmured. "I wish we could have it now." Chuckling, he added,

"But I have to be patient, I know."

David wrapped his arms around Isaac and held him close. "Yes. It seems you'll have to wait."

Then he had an idea.

Chapter Two

"F A LA LA la la!" Anna's voice rang out from the front hallway.

"Come on in," Aaron called as Anna and Lola bustled into the living room carrying bags stuffed with sparkly decorations.

David blinked at his sister. "Anna—your hair! It's…"

She turned her head side to side as she ran her hand over her chopped blond hair. "Short? It's called a… Lola, what's it called?"

"A bob," Lola answered. She'd taken Anna under her wing. Lola's brown hair was cut in the same short style, but she had a streak of outrageous color through it that was currently green and was different almost every time David saw her. He was secretly relieved Anna's hair wasn't colored. Since she'd turned eighteen and left Zebulon that summer, she'd found work as a live-in nanny and housekeeper for a wealthy family. David didn't think they'd be too pleased if she came home with strange hair. Maybe he was old-fashioned, but Anna's golden hair was lovely the way it was.

Anna bit her lip. "Do you like it, David?"

He realized he was staring. "Of course! It looks very pretty." He held out his arms for a hug and gave Anna a squeeze. "I've just never seen you with short hair."

She stepped back and shrugged. "I figured it's been six months since I've been living English, and it was time to shake things up."

Aaron and Isaac came through the dining room carrying bowls of snacks. They greeted Lola and hugged Anna, complimenting her haircut. David couldn't help wondering what Mother would think of Anna's hair. She certainly wouldn't like it.

The pang of longing that accompanied any thoughts of his mother and other sisters back in Zebulon sank through him heavily. It had been a couple of months since they'd had any letters from either of their families. They worried, but at least their English friend June lived close to Zebulon and would tell them if anything bad happened.

He pushed the thoughts away. It hurt far too much to think of his family in Zebulon. All he could do was focus on his new family. He kissed Isaac lightly, and Isaac gave him a quizzical smile.

"Okay?" Isaac murmured.

"Mmm-hmm. Just happy." It was mostly true.

"Isaac, I brought you that book we have to read for history. I finished it, so you don't have to buy it now." Lola fished a paperback out of one of her bags.

"Awesome, thanks." Isaac peered at the book. "I'm going to wait until after Christmas to read it. World War II was really sad. There's so much stuff we never learned about at all growing up."

Aaron snorted. "Yeah, hard to learn much when they want to keep us ignorant of anything except Amish ways." He shook his head. "Let's not talk about that, or I'll just end up on my soapbox, and no one wants that. Let's get this decorating party started."

Aaron offered him a beer, but David took a soda. Although he didn't drink to numb himself anymore, he was careful not to slip back into old habits. As Anna shrugged out of her hoodie, David noticed her shirt was rather low-cut, just like Lola's. Anna was quite slim and didn't have as much to show off as Lola, yet somehow her chest looked bigger than usual. Maybe it was one of those pushy bras that girls wore sometimes.

Isaac followed his gaze and smirked before tugging David with him into the bright kitchen. "If you keep frowning so much your face will stay that way."

David chuckled. "But don't you think that shirt is a little..." He sighed. "I don't want boys getting the wrong idea about my sister."

"Anna's not dumb, David. Jen gave her the

whole safe-sex talk. Besides, she's eighteen. When I was eighteen, you were having sex with me. I'm only nineteen now. So why shouldn't she go out with boys and wear what she wants?"

"I know, I know." David picked up a tray of cookies Aaron had baked. They made the whole town house smell like butter and chocolate, and he couldn't resist taking a bite. "She's still my baby sister. What if it was Katie dating English boys?"

It was Isaac's turn to frown. "I see your point."

"I just don't want her to get hurt." His other sisters were out of his reach back in Zebulon, and he had to trust that his mother's new husband was taking care of them. For so many years after his father had died, David had been responsible for his family. It was only Anna with him now, and he wouldn't let her down. "But you're right—she's a smart girl. She always has been. And her hair does look very nice."

"It does. This isn't a time for worrying. It's for spreading Christmas cheer for all to hear."

"Are you going to start singing?" David grinned. There was a television channel that seemed to play only holiday movies, and they'd watched one every night that week.

"I might." Isaac plucked a cookie off the tray and beamed. "Our very first English Christmas."

David smiled and gave him a soft kiss. "Maybe next year we can do our own tree in our very own house."

Aaron breezed into the kitchen, his bare feet slapping on the pale hardwood floor. With his blue eyes and light blond hair, he and Isaac didn't look much alike, but their smiles were the same. "Speaking of which, no luck with the house hunt?" Aaron washed his hands at the sink and wiped them on his jeans before going to work chopping carrots and peppers for a vegetable tray.

Isaac and David shook their heads.

"Well, you know you're welcome to stay here as long as you want."

"But you're not charging us nearly enough for rent," Isaac replied. "You wouldn't believe how much these places are."

"Oh, I believe it." Aaron grimaced. "Prices are insane in the Bay Area. And yes, we're charging you plenty considering we don't want to charge you anything at all. Isaac, you and David have been working your asses off building furniture." He chopped a red pepper into strips with quick movements.

David wondered what Mrs. Byler would think if she saw how skilled her son was in the kitchen. Would she be completely horrified, or maybe just a little bit proud?

Aaron went on. "You guys paid us back for the stuff we bought you when you first came here, and your rent is more than enough. Save your money."

He scraped the vegetables onto the tray with his knife. "Can you grab the dips from the fridge and then help me bring in the tree?"

Pine needles scratched David's face as he helped haul the tree in from outside and fasten it into a stand in front of the big picture window in the living room that overlooked the steep street. They all stood back and admired it.

"Good thing we brought extra decorations," Lola noted. "That is one mofo of a Christmas tree."

"Yep." Aaron grinned. "Jen and I always just did a little tree, but we're going all out this year. Too bad she had to cover a shift at the hospital. It'll be a nice surprise for when she gets home."

As they went to work untangling the strands of colored bulbs, Lola asked, "So what's Amish Christmas like? Guess it's slightly less flashy and consumer-based."

They all laughed, and Isaac held his finger and thumb apart. "Just a *tiny* bit. No tree or decorations, and hardly any presents. Usually my parents put candy in our shoes. That was it. I mean, we didn't have any decorations in our houses normally, so there was definitely nothing special going up at Christmas. We were supposed to be thinking about Jesus and everything." He quickly added, "Not that I won't think about Jesus on Christmas this year."

Aaron clapped a hand on Isaac's shoulder. "Don't worry, little brother. You can enjoy all the decorations and gifts and fun stuff about Christmas. I'm sure God won't mind. And even though I'm not religious anymore, it's a cultural holiday, and I can still enjoy all the fun stuff too. It's a win-win."

"So I guess there was no Santa Claus coming down the chimney in Amish country?" Lola asked.

"I had no idea who Santa was," Anna said. "I didn't really understand it until last month; the kids were delighted to explain it all in great detail. They are very concerned with being on the nice list. Oh, I forgot to tell you that the Parkers said I can have the whole week off at Christmas, so I can come and stay if that's okay? I won't know what to do with myself without a house to clean and kids to chase."

Aaron winked. "Don't worry, we'll put you to work. You can help me make the pies. Shoofly, apple, and maybe strawberry if we can find some good ones. Jen's family will love them."

"We're going to have pie?" David smiled at the thought. "That'll make it seem more like home."

"So you didn't have decorations or a tree or presents, but you had pie?" Lola asked. "Hard to go wrong with pie."

"We had a huge feast," Isaac answered. "That's really what Christmas was about. Going visiting and having roast and pie and candy. So much food. On Christmas and Old Christmas too."

Lola's brows drew together as she triumphantly untangled a line of lights and passed them to Aaron.

"Wait, what's Old Christmas?"

"January sixth," Isaac said. "We'd fast in the mornings, and it was more…serious, I guess. We did still get to have pie and a big dinner later."

"On regular Christmas, David would always make us little toys and hide them under our beds." Anna gave him a smile as she unrolled a long, glittering red rope that was called a garland according to its package.

Aaron turned on the TV and flipped through the channels. "There. The perfect accompaniment to tree trimming."

David peered at the screen. It showed a fireplace with burning wood, and…that was it. Bells jingled in the merry song playing. He looked at Isaac, who appeared as confused as David felt. "Is that…a show?" David asked.

"They do it at the holidays every year," Aaron explained. "It's just supposed to be on in the background."

"Huh." Isaac tilted his head. "It's kind of nice." A new song started, and he said, "Oh, we sang this one at church last week! Remember, David? It was really fun."

David nodded with a smile. As he took the lid off a box of ice-blue ornaments, he hummed "Joy to the World" along with Isaac. It was quite a change from the German dirges they'd sung at Amish church. Their Unitarian church was so much fun, and no one minded that he and Isaac were gay. David had never thought he'd actually look forward to Sundays.

They ate and laughed and sang as they decorated the tree. When they finished, it was covered in lights, garlands, glittering decorations, and strings of silver called tinsel. Aaron gave Isaac the star to put on top, and then they turned off the lamps in the living room. It was dark but for the pale glow of the streetlights outside as Aaron got down on his hands and knees to plug in the tree's lights.

The tree burst into glorious life with red, green, blue, yellow, and pink lights strung around it and a sparkling star on top. David couldn't stop a little gasp, and Anna clapped while Isaac grinned from ear to ear.

"It's almost like magic!" Isaac exclaimed.

It was the most vain, worldly thing David had ever seen, and here it was right in the living room. In the tree's rainbow glow, David watched his Isaac laugh joyfully, and it was *glorious*.

"HEY." JEN SMILED wanly as she shuffled into the living room in her scrubs and fuzzy slippers. Her long dark curls were knotted on her head, and she yawned widely before noticing the tree. "Oh my God! You guys, that looks amazing. I love it!"

Isaac grinned. Jen worked so hard, and he loved

seeing her happy. Anna and Lola had left before it got too late, and now David, Isaac, and Aaron were sprawled on the sectional couch. Jen leaned over to kiss Aaron lightly as he paused the movie.

"Tough day in the ER?" Aaron asked, rubbing her hip.

"Long-ass day involving too many people who don't wear their damn seat belts. But I see you guys were very productive. Strong work." She stretched her arms over her head. "Oh, my mom wants to make sure you boys and Anna are coming for Christmas Eve. I assured her you wouldn't miss a chance to eat her chicken adobo."

"We'd definitely never miss that," David answered.

Aaron grinned. "I've already regaled them with tales of Filipino Christmas and the culinary delights to be discovered."

"All right, I'm going to go upstairs and watch the latest episode of *The Bachelor* or something equally ridiculous." She gave a wave as she headed through the dining room.

"Your dinner's on the counter. Just nuke it for a minute," Aaron called after her.

Isaac and David shared a glance, and Isaac said loudly, "You can watch your program down here, Jen. We don't mind."

She popped her head back around the corner. "That's okay, sweetie. I need some alone time."

David frowned. "But…"

"It's fine." Aaron waved a hand dismissively and pressed the remote. The screech of rubber tires on pavement filled the room as the police in the movie chased the bank robbers.

Lowering his voice, Isaac murmured, "But it's her house. She shouldn't have to go upstairs to watch TV."

Aaron insisted, "She *wants* to go upstairs. You heard her—she needs some alone time."

Jen passed by in the hallway with her plate and a bottle of beer. "Night."

When she was gone, David said, "She needs alone time because we're here too much."

"What?" Aaron shook his head. "No, it's because she's tired and wants to be alone. If it was just me here, she would have done exactly the same thing. Trust me. She's surrounded by people at the hospital, and she needs to be alone for a bit to recharge her batteries. She's an extroverted introvert. It's got nothing to do with you guys."

"Okay," Isaac said, making a mental note to look up "extrovert" and "introvert" later. "If you're sure."

"Positive."

As they watched cars explode and plummet off a bridge, Isaac couldn't get it off his mind. He could sense David's tension beside him too. It had been almost a year that they'd been living with Aaron and Jen. They'd never once made Isaac and David feel unwelcome, but Isaac knew they'd all be happier living apart. Just the other day, David had come home with a migraine. The city was so noisy, and David loved his peace and quiet.

Isaac couldn't get the house they'd seen the day before out of his head. If only the rent was a little less, they could do without some things to afford it. It hadn't even been fancy—there were lots of things that needed to be fixed in both the houses Margery had shown them. Isaac made a mental list of all the things he'd fix up if they were his houses.

Then he had an idea.

Chapter Three

F ROM THE CORNER of his eye, David saw Anna poking her head into the workshop. He waved before pulling out his earplugs and tapping Isaac, who was bent over a long board, sticking out his tongue in concentration as he measured the marks for cutting.

Isaac straightened up and pulled out his earbuds. "Hey, Anna."

She grimaced as she came into the concrete rectangle and shut the door behind her. "Wow. Is it always this loud?"

David nodded grimly. "It's gotten worse and worse." His neighbor's music *thump, thump, thumped* through the wall and seemed to reverberate in the air like a living creature. Most of the other garages down the alley stored cars, but he had the terrible luck to be next to a man who repaired engines to the so-called tune of the loudest music David had ever heard. He'd asked many times to have it turned down, and the next day it was inevitably shaking the foundation again.

"It wouldn't be so bad if it was pretty," Isaac said. "I thought songs were supposed to have melodies and stuff." He picked up his phone. "I've got some great songs on here I can listen to, at least. I try to drown it out."

David wished he could, but it drove him just as crazy blasting music in his ears, so he stuck with the earplugs. Even with the orange foam squeezed into his ears, he could feel the heavy beat of the music and hear it faintly.

Anna put her hands in the pockets of her red raincoat. "Well, I hope you can find somewhere else to work soon." She scuffed the toe of her sneaker on the concrete, pushing sawdust back and forth. "So…"

David cringed. "What? I know that tone. What did you do?"

"Nothing!" Her cheeks pinked up. "I swear. But I have a favor to ask. Of both of you."

David and Isaac shared a glance. "Okay." David waited, his muscles rigid.

"Well, I was thinking maybe you could take a couple hours off and we could go shopping? There's a mall we can take the bus to. I need your help finding gifts for Aaron and Jen." She raised her hands. "I know, I know, we're not supposed to be spending our money on gifts, but I want to get you all a little something and wrap up the boxes with sparkly paper and put them under the tree on Christmas. And I know you both got me something even though we said no gifts."

David and Isaac shared another glance. "How did you know?" Isaac asked.

She smirked. "I didn't for sure, but I figured. So will you come? Lola can't, and it's Christmas Eve."

Sighing, David hung up his saw on its hook on the wall. "I wouldn't go to the mall on Christmas Eve for anyone but you." There'd been a story about it on the news that morning saying how busy it would be.

As they fought through a surge of bodies an hour later trying to get out of Macy's, David concentrated on long inhales and exhales. He hadn't had a panic attack in months, but sweat prickled the back of his neck, and his heart raced.

He didn't know how there could be this many people in San Francisco, let alone this many of them crammed inside one mall at one time. Christmas carols filled the air, along with the buzzing drone of the crowds, people with desperate, hungry faces striding from store to store.

"Okay?" Isaac murmured, snagging David's hand.

"Yeah." David blew out a long breath. "It's hot in here." He tugged at the collar of his hoodie.

"I know." Isaac called ahead, "Anna, are you

almost done?"

"Almost." She grinned. "We're getting the full English Christmas experience."

"We're going to the bathroom," Isaac said, tugging David's hand. "We'll meet you by the pretzels down there."

"Isaac, I'm fine," David protested, but he let Isaac lead him down a hallway and inside an empty and surprisingly clean bathroom. Considering he'd used an outhouse for years, he shouldn't have been picky anyway.

Isaac ushered David into a stall and pressed him against the door, kissing him gently. "Hey," he whispered.

"Hey." David exhaled with a smile. "I'm okay, Isaac. I'm not going to freak out. It's crowded and noisy, but… I'm okay. It's not like it was when we first came here. I can handle it."

"I know." Isaac brushed their lips together again. "I needed a break too. Let's just catch our breath for a minute."

David nodded gratefully, and for minutes they simply held each other, breathing in and out as other men came and went. David's pulse slowed, and soon he felt fortified and ready to go back out and face the mall. But Isaac didn't seem to be in any rush, so what was a few more minutes? He snuck his hands under Isaac's sweater, tracing his fingers over the skin of Isaac's lower back.

Shivering, Isaac kissed him again, sliding his tongue between David's lips. The outer door of the bathroom opened, and they kissed as the man went about his business at the urinal. When they were alone again, David chuckled. "We shouldn't be doing this. Too many people around."

"We're not doing anything." Isaac smiled slyly. "Although I heard that lots of gay men have sex in bathrooms like this. They call it 'cruising.' I don't know why, but they do."

David pondered it. "So, are you cruising with me, Isaac Byler?" The stress and tension of the crowds seemed miles away here in their private little corner.

Isaac grinned. "Maybe I am. You interested, David Lantz?"

He dipped his hands below Isaac's waist, squeezing his round ass. "Always."

Biting his lip, Isaac said, "I guess we shouldn't be in here too long, though."

"Hmm. Guess not." Their eyes were locked, and tremors of desire rippled through David. They hadn't had to hide and be quiet for so long, and excitement ran hot in his veins.

Apparently in Isaac's too. "Maybe you should fuck me in here. Up against the wall."

A little boy's voice rang out. "Daddy, I can go myself! I'm a big boy!"

"Okay, you do it by yourself," a man said, chuckling.

With Isaac rigid against him, David held his breath. He felt the flush all the way to the tips of his ears as he and Isaac stared at each other in horror. They waited for what seemed a terribly long time while the child went to the bathroom and then washed his hands so thoroughly he could have been a doctor on one of the medical shows on TV.

When they were finally alone again, they burst out laughing and quickly hurried out of the stall. "Uh, we'll finish that later at home," David muttered as he washed his hands.

Isaac nodded vigorously and wrinkled his nose. "Cruising isn't all it's cracked up to be."

By the pretzel store, they looked for Anna, peering at endless faces that rushed by. David frowned. "She should be here by now."

"Oh, there! She's waving." Isaac headed into the center of the mall where a fancy house sat. It looked like it was made of gingerbread, and in front of it was a man in a Santa suit sitting on a plush red throne.

"Hurry! It's almost our turn." Anna waved them over. When they looked at the line snaking out behind her, they hesitated. "It's okay. I told them I was saving your spot."

As they joined the line, David watched a little girl climb onto Santa's knee. "Almost our turn for what?"

"Pictures with Santa. They print them out right over there. We get two poses, so one with me on

Santa's lap, and then one with you two."

"Us two…on his lap?" Isaac exclaimed. "We're too heavy."

A young woman dressed in a short red dress with fuzzy white trim ushered them forward. "Adults do it all the time. Santa can handle it. Come on, you're up."

Beaming, Anna skipped up to Santa and plopped on his knee. They had a conversation David couldn't hear, then smiled widely for the photographer. Then the woman in red was urging them up the three steps to the throne.

"Uh…" David waved at the man. "Hi."

"Ho, ho, ho! Merry Christmas!" The older man patted his meaty thighs. "Have a seat and tell me if you've been naughty or nice."

With a helpless glance at each other, they did as they were told, David perching as gingerly as he could so they didn't crush the poor man.

"Um, mostly nice," Isaac answered with a blush.

"Your sister tells me this is your first Christmas here in San Francisco."

"Yes," David said. "Where we're from, Christmas isn't like this."

"And what do you want Santa to bring you?"

David and Isaac looked at each other, and Isaac said, "A house would be really nice."

The man barked out a laugh. "Wouldn't it?"

"But as long as we have each other, we don't

need anything else," David added.

"Geez, you guys should get a job with Hallmark." Santa laughed. "Okay, say cheese!"

When they went back for their set of pictures twenty minutes later, David stared at the images of Anna with her infectious grin, and he and Isaac laughing with Santa. In Zebulon, mirrors hadn't even been allowed, never mind pictures. He could imagine how their parents would frown, the bishop and preachers wagging their fingers and sermonizing about the vain, worldly sinfulness of it all.

"Let's go buy picture frames," he said, taking Isaac and Anna's hands and battling the crowds with a smile.

Chapter Four

"I ATE TOO MUCH." Aaron groaned as they trooped up the stairs to the town house.

"That's what Christmas is all about, babe." Jen grimaced. "But yeah. Me too. My family thinks we're all too skinny. Good thing I don't have to work for two whole days. I'll need that time to digest. And we haven't even had turkey yet. I'd say we should throw out all the leftovers my aunties packed for us, but let's be real. We're going to eat them for breakfast."

Isaac grinned. "I'm sure we'll make room by then." He was full too, but the food was so delicious.

As they took off their shoes in the foyer, Anna asked, "Do we have cookies to leave out for Santa? I was told this is very important if you want presents under the tree and nice things in your stocking. Apparently some kids get bits of coal? That would actually be useful where we grew up. Not really here."

The stockings were hung from the shelf below

the TV on the wall. The red, velvety fabric of each stocking bore their names in glittering letters, and maybe it was silly, but it made Isaac feel special. He knew Santa Claus wasn't real, yet the idea that when they came downstairs in the morning the stockings would be full and there'd be more presents under the tree put a grin on his face. Especially when he thought about the surprise he had for David.

As the others talked about Santa and what exactly a sugarplum was, Isaac slipped out and carefully prepared his surprise. Then he caught sight of the pile of mail on the little hall table, realizing he hadn't checked it since the day before. His heart kicked up as he went through the flyers and a few bills, hoping to see a plain white envelope with familiar scratchy handwriting.

"Anything?" David asked quietly, making Isaac jump.

Isaac tried to keep his voice light. "Only if you're interested in a sale on diapers."

"Well, not yet. Maybe one day." He rubbed Isaac's back.

Maybe one day. But how would they ever be able to have a baby? Adoption wasn't easy, and who knew—

"What's going on in there?" David tapped Isaac's head softly.

Pushing away the useless worries of the future, Isaac put the mail back on the table. "Nothing. I guess… I guess I was hoping for a letter. It would be so nice to hear from my brothers and Katie." Not to mention his parents, but he knew better than to hope for that. Still, it hurt.

"I know. Anna and I didn't get any letter either." David sighed. "Our first Christmas without them. It seems impossible, though. How was it only a year ago that we were still living in Zebulon, and you and I were…" Shuddering, he held Isaac's face in his hands and kissed him. "I'm so glad we're here together."

"Me too," Isaac whispered. Last Christmas they hadn't even been speaking, and Isaac had never been so incredibly unhappy. "We can't control what happens in Zebulon. But we're together, and we have Aaron and Jen, and Anna, and all our friends." He hugged David tightly. "We have so much."

"We do." David leaned back. "As long as I have you, it doesn't matter where we live."

Isaac's belly fluttered—he could tell David now. It was after midnight, after all. After they set out the cookies and a glass of milk, everyone was ready for bed. As the others went up, Isaac lingered in the foyer.

David glanced back. "Isaac?"

Aaron had left the Christmas tree on, and the colored lights from the living room spilled into the darkness of the foyer. Isaac pointed to David's shoes. "You'd better check in there."

David smiled. "Candy? I suppose I can squeeze in a piece."

"Look and see."

Crouching down, David checked the empty shoe first. Then he stuck his hand into the other sneaker and pulled out the key ring. It was just plain silver since Isaac hadn't had time to buy a different one. Two keys hung from it, and David stood as he peered at them.

"Keys to what?"

Isaac's stomach clenched, and his heart thumped. Maybe this hadn't been a good idea. He and David had made a pact that they'd always make decisions together, and he'd gone ahead and done this without saying a word. "Well… It's the key to that house," he blurted.

David stared at the keys in his hand.

"The house in Dublin? With the perfect garage and everything?"

David blinked at Isaac. "But how?"

The words tripped out. "I called Margery and asked her if we could do work for her. Fix things on the houses and in exchange pay less rent. If we fixed up that other house with the basement apartment, she could charge more for it. And we could help with her house too, since her husband can't do repairs anymore."

"How much is the rent?"

"Twenty-two hundred. I asked for two thousand.

She wanted more, but I think we can afford it, David. I really do. I used the money for Florida and a little from our joint account. I know I should have asked you first, but I wanted it to be a surprise for Christmas. She said I only had to give her one month up front, and we'll have a one-month trial and see if we're all happy with the deal. So we can always find another place if we don't like it." Isaac stopped talking, and his heartbeat was loud in his ears.

David was still staring at him. "She agreed to only one month up front?"

He flushed. "I told her we were Amish, so I guess she thinks we're trustworthy. You know how English people are. They think Amish never lie or do bad things."

"We can move into that house? When?"

"As soon as we like. Officially it's January first, but she said we can go over anytime. I figured we can see how it goes before you give notice on your workshop downtown. Make sure we like it first."

"Isaac…" David opened and closed his mouth.

"Are you mad? I should have talked to you. I just wanted to give you a surprise and—"

David kissed him hard, crushing their mouths together as he hauled Isaac close. Isaac gripped David's arms, and they kissed and kissed until they were both panting.

Isaac blinked. "You're not mad?"

"*Eechel*, I love you so much," David said with a

wide smile.

The little nickname—*acorn* in their Amish German dialect—never failed to make Isaac glow all the way to his toes. "I love you too, my David."

"Oh, Isaac. I can't believe this. I wish we could go see the house right now and start planning."

He grinned. "And the first thing to plan is what our bed will look like."

"Well, actually…" He tugged Isaac's hand and led him to the sliding glass doors that opened to the narrow backyard.

The stones of the patio were cold under Isaac's socks, but he didn't care as he noticed the tarp covering something by the fence. "What's that?"

Biting his lip, David pulled off the tarp.

Isaac squinted in the darkness, the moon too thin to give much light. He went closer, reaching out to run his fingers over the plastic Bubble Wrap. There were large pieces of wood securely wrapped, and as he tried to make sense of their shapes, he realized the tall one under his hand was a bedpost.

"David! Is this… Did you?" Isaac's jaw dropped. "Is this our bed?"

"I know we said we'd design it together, but I wanted to surprise you, and I think I know what you like."

"We said no gifts." He teased, "What happened to the gloves?"

"I think Santa might put them in your stocking.

Besides, you didn't stick to it either." David swung the keys on his finger.

"Yeah, but that's for both of us." Isaac stared at the bed frame. Although it was hard to tell for sure in the darkness, it seemed to be made of the dark cherry wood that Isaac loved. His breath caught as David pressed against him from behind, his arms stealing around Isaac's middle.

"This is for both of us too." His warm breath sent a shiver down Isaac's spine. "I can't wait to have you in this bed."

Isaac's mouth went dry as his body tingled. "Uh-huh. That'll be good. Let's do that right now."

David laughed, squeezing Isaac tighter. "It's all ready to be put together, but I suppose we'll have to wait until we move in."

"How did you get it back here? When?"

"This morning. I've been building it nonstop whenever you weren't at the workshop. Our noisy neighbor was surprisingly helpful and let me store the pieces there. He had a pickup truck he let me borrow too." David pulled a folded piece of paper from his pocket. "And here—this is what it'll look like."

Isaac shifted his feet on the chilly stones as he peered at the drawing of a wooden bed with a gently curved headboard with serpentine slats and round knobs on the four posts. "I… Wow. Wow."

David turned Isaac in his arms, a frown creasing his face. "Was it the wrong thing to do? If you don't like it, if it's not what you'd imagined, I can sell it, and we'll build another one."

"Don't you dare sell my bed." Isaac cupped David's cheek, the stubble rough on his palm as he kissed him. "It's perfect. Just perfect."

David leaned their foreheads together. "I wish we could see the house again now. There are so many plans to make."

Isaac's pulse raced. "Why can't we? You have your license now, and Aaron said we can borrow his car anytime. The roads will be so quiet now. We'll get there in no time. I'll leave a note, but we'll be back before long."

Nodding, David's eyes gleamed in the night. "Let's see our new home."

THE ONLY TIME DAVID had ever experienced the city so still was when he and Isaac had arrived off the bus all the way from Minnesota in the middle of the night. Tonight there was no fog as they drove the sleeping streets, and even the freeway seemed empty. Christmas lights shone from houses and businesses, and Isaac found a radio station playing carols.

As they approached Dublin, "Silent Night" filled the car, and a few snowflakes drifted down, quickly melting on the windshield.

"All is calm; all is bright."

Isaac had the map on his phone, and David followed his quiet directions. When they pulled into the empty driveway, he shut off the engine, and they stared at the house in silence as a song about a good king played.

"I used to daydream about sharing a house with you," Isaac murmured. "How we'd work together in the barn, eat lunch in our kitchen, and sleep in our own bed at night, safe and warm together under a pretty quilt. And I know this won't be like that, but it'll be ours, David. At least for now."

David had to swallow hard over the lump in his throat. He reached for Isaac's hand. "I dreamed of that too. Who would have thought we'd end up here?"

Isaac squeezed his fingers. "Sometimes I miss it. Miss *them*, mostly. But having this with you makes it all worth it." A smile brightened his face. "Come on."

David had put the keys in his pocket, so he was the one to unlock the door and take a tentative step inside. The wooden floor creaked under his sneakers. "Where's the light?"

Isaac brushed past him. "Hold on. Close your eyes."

He did as he was told.

"Okay. Open."

A little gasp escaped David's lips. Someone had strung Christmas lights through the entryway and into the living room and down the hall to the kitchen. "When?"

"Anna helped me this morning." Isaac shut the door behind David before frowning. "Uh-oh. Don't move."

"What?" David glanced down at his feet but didn't see anything amiss.

Isaac was still frowning. "It's up there."

Tipping his head back, David peered at the ceiling. There was a gold-trimmed light fixture above him with something hanging from it. A branch? Berries? "What is that?"

"I think it's called mistletoe." A little smile lifted Isaac's lips.

"Oh, like in that movie?" David realized what Isaac was playing at and tried to hide his own smile. He cleared his throat. "This is a very serious English tradition from what I understand. If you're caught under the mistletoe, you have to kiss, or there are terrible consequences."

Isaac nodded gravely. "Terrible. We'd better not take any chances."

Their noses bumped in the low light, and they laughed, their lips meeting and teasing. David leaned their foreheads together. "We should have mistletoe up all year long."

"Mmm." Isaac lowered his head and sucked on the sensitive skin of David's neck as his hands roamed.

"Isaac, we're barely in the front door. Shouldn't we look at the rest of the—" Isaac cupped David's cock through his jeans, and David moaned. "Although it's not going anywhere."

"I think I'd better kiss you again. Just to make sure we didn't do anything wrong with the mistletoe."

"We can't be too careful. It would be bad luck." He tried to capture Isaac's mouth, but Isaac sank to his knees. Isaac went to work on David's jeans while he looked up through his lashes, and David's pulse leapt.

"Better kiss you more than one place," Isaac whispered.

"It's tradition."

"Yep. This is totally what English people do under the mistletoe." Isaac's breath ghosted over David's groin as he freed his cock.

David shivered and ran his thumb over Isaac's lips. "So beautiful."

Isaac took him into his mouth, holding David's hips and sucking gently. David leaned back against the front door, moaning as Isaac took him deeper. From where he stood, David could almost see the whole little house, lit by the colored fairy lights. The two bedrooms were dark beyond their open doors, and there were so many plans to make.

David thumped his head against the door as Isaac sucked harder and caressed his balls. Isaac licked and teased, and David ran his fingers through Isaac's hair, petting him. In the hush of the small hours in the colorful glow, David thought he must have been dreaming. Sometimes it didn't seem true that he could actually be so lucky.

Their life in Zebulon seemed years ago and a million miles away. He'd never thought he'd be able to leave—never thought he'd be able to love Isaac openly. It hadn't been easy, but here they were in their *own house*. It didn't matter that they didn't own it, or that it wasn't where they'd spend the rest of their lives. For now, it was perfect.

He found himself smiling between the gasps of pleasure that escaped his lips. He hoped all English Christmases would be this magical.

Isaac nuzzled David's balls while David stroked his hair, a swell of pure affection choking him. It didn't take long until he was coming down Isaac's throat with a cry he didn't have to muffle this time. When Isaac got to his feet, David kissed him deeply, tasting himself.

Isaac leaned back. "Come on. Let's see our house."

But David spun Isaac around, pushing him against the door with a lingering kiss before he sank to his knees. "That can wait." He pointed to the mistletoe. "It'll be our tradition."

As he took Isaac between his lips, Isaac's laughter turned to cries of pleasure that echoed through the empty rooms, soon to be filled with so much love.

About the Author

Keira aims for the perfect mix of character, plot, and heat in her M/M romances. She writes everything from swashbuckling pirates to heartwarming holiday escapism. Her fave tropes are enemies to lovers, age gaps, forced proximity, and passionate virgins. Although she loves delicious angst along the way, Keira guarantees happy endings!

Discover more at:
KeiraAndrews.com